THE ROAD TO EL DORADO

ALTIVO'S ADVENTURE

adapted from the screenplay by
SUE KASSIRER

DREAMWORKS ™

GOLD AND GLORY
THE ROAD TO
EL DORADO

A special thanks to Corinne Antoniades, Alex Bell,
and Scott McPhail for their invaluable assistance with this book.

PUFFIN BOOKS
Published by the Penguin Group
Penguin Putnam Books for Young Readers,
345 Hudson Street, New York, New York 10014, U.S.A.
Penguin Books Ltd, 27 Wrights Lane, London W8 5TZ, England
Penguin Books Australia Ltd, Ringwood, Victoria, Australia
Penguin Books Canada Ltd, 10 Alcorn Avenue, Toronto, Ontario, Canada M4V 3B2
Penguin Books (N.Z.) Ltd, 182-190 Wairau Road, Auckland 10, New Zealand

Penguin Books Ltd, Registered Offices: Harmondsworth, Middlesex, England

Published by Puffin Books, a division of Penguin Putnam Books for Young Readers, 2000

1 3 5 7 9 10 8 6 4 2

TM & © 2000 DreamWorks
All rights reserved

ISBN 0-14-130711-0

Printed in the United States of America

CONTENTS

Chapter One: A Proud Warhorse 5

Chapter Two: The Dice Game 9

Chapter Three: On Board 15

Chapter Four: A Smart Horse 19

Chapter Five: Overboard! 23

Chapter Six: A Losing Battle 27

Chapter Seven: Rescued! 31

Chapter Eight: Lost at Sea 35

Chapter Nine: "It's Laaaaand!" 39

Chapter Ten: The Map 43

Chapter Eleven: Through the Jungle 49

Chapter Twelve: A Great Big Rock 57

Chapter Thirteen: El Dorado! 61

CHAPTER ONE

A PROUD WARHORSE

A gleaming white horse rode proudly through the streets of Madrid. He held his head high and he looked noble, indeed. Why wouldn't he? On his back sat one of Spain's most famous explorers. On his back sat his master, the fierce Hernan Cortes.

"Today we sail to the New World! For Spain! For glory! For gold!" Cortes raised a cup high in a toast.

"*Viva* Cortes! Long live Cortes!" the crowd yelled as their hero rode by.

KABOOM! KABOOM KABOOM! Cortes's soldiers fired three shots into the air to celebrate.

Startled, the strong white horse reared—and spilled the great explorer's wine all over his fine clothes.

"Argh! Altivo, eyes forward!" yelled Cortes.

Altivo was embarrassed, but what could he do?

He had been trained to defend his master when shots rang out. He simply could not get used to the sound of rifles fired in celebration. But he decided he would try harder next time. After all, he wanted to please his master.

Yes, Altivo would do his best to help Cortes find his gold. For that was Altivo's job. But he simply did not understand humans and their love of gold. Why was it so important to them? It shined. It glistened. So what?

As a small colt, Altivo had been trained as a warhorse. So had his father before him and even his grandfather. Altivo was proud of his family and proud of his mission. But sometimes he would look at other horses—sporting horses, show horses, carriage horses—and he would wonder what their lives were like.

Or he would look at people playing games and having fun. True, they probably didn't have as much gold and glory as his master, Cortes. But they seemed to have something else. They smiled more. They laughed. They looked happy.

Just then, Altivo spotted two carefree-looking young men. They were rolling dice on the ground and laughing and singing. One of them picked up a mandolin and began strumming it. How Altivo longed to join in on the fun!

CHAPTER TWO

THE DICE GAME

Altivo watched the two men playing with the dice. It's true, they were having fun, but they were also cheating! They were using special trick dice. Every time they rolled them, the number they wanted would come up. They were winning lots of money this way.

"Seven!" called Tulio, a thin, dark-haired man.

"All right!" cried his blond partner, Miguel. They slapped one another a high-five, laughed, and sang at the top of their lungs, "Tons of gold for you—hey! Tons of gold for me—hey! Tons of gold for we . . ."

Pretty soon the sailors had lost all their money to Tulio and Miguel.

"HEY!" barked Zaragoza, a huge, gruff-looking sailor. "One more roll."

"Uh, guys, you're broke! You got nothing to bet

with!" Tulio pointed out to the sailor.

"Oh, yeah?" growled Zaragoza. "I got this!" He reached into his jacket and pulled out an old, rolled-up piece of paper. "A map of the wonders of the New World!"

"Well! Let's have a look," said Miguel. He grabbed the map and pulled Tulio over by his side. "Tulio, look! El Dorado! The city of gold! This could be our destiny! Our fate!"

"If I believed in fate, I wouldn't be playing with loaded dice!" Tulio answered. He didn't want to play for a silly map.

But Miguel made a pleading face. He looked so sad and so hopeful. Altivo could tell that Tulio couldn't say no to that face.

Tulio shrugged, turned to the large sailor, and

said, "All right, Pee Wee. You're on!"

"Not with those," said Zaragoza, pointing at Miguel and Tulio's trick dice. "This time we use *my* dice!"

Tulio gulped. "I am going to kill you!" he whispered to Miguel. Without their trick dice, they could lose everything they had just won!

All eyes were fixed on the two little dice as Tulio rolled them across the stone floor.

Altivo held his breath.

"Seven!" yelled Tulio. Lucky seven—they won again! And this time they really were lucky. They weren't even cheating.

"All right!" shouted Miguel. He and Tulio eagerly gathered up the gold coins and the map they had won.

Zaragoza picked up something as well—the old dice. He looked at them carefully. "Hmmm . . . I knew it!" he said. "Your dice are loaded!"

"What?" cried Tulio, staring at Miguel. "You gave me loaded dice?" He turned to go, but a large policeman stepped in front of him.

"He was the one who was cheating!" shouted Miguel. "Arrest him! He tricked these sailors and took their money!"

"Oh, now I'm the thief?" asked Tulio.

"Yes!" answered Miguel.

"Take a look in the mirror, pal!" shouted Tulio.

"You'd better give them their money back or I'll . . ."
Miguel grabbed a sword from a guard. "En garde!"
he cried, pointing it at Tulio.

Tulio snatched a sword from another guard, and
he and Miguel raised their weapons. Back and forth
they fought, leaping through the air and swinging
their swords wildly.

Finally, Miguel pressed his sword against Tulio's
chest. Altivo watched, fearing for Tulio's life. But
then Tulio stood up and announced, "Ladies and
gentlemen, we've decided it's a draw!"

"Thank you all for coming!" added Miguel as he
took a bow.

"*Adios!*" shouted Tulio, and with that the two

friends tossed their swords away, leaped over a wall—and ran for their lives!

Cortes touched Altivo's flanks lightly with his spurs, and they trotted off toward their waiting ship. Duty beckoned, and Altivo obeyed. After all, he was a serious warhorse, with no time for playing games!

But the thought of the two men laughing and having fun and adventures together stayed with him. And for the first time ever, the proud warhorse wondered what it would be like to just have fun.

CHAPTER THREE

ON BOARD

Back on Cortes's ship, Altivo stood proudly in the bright sunlight as several sailors washed him down and groomed him. They brushed his coat until it gleamed like sunlit snow. They carefully combed and styled his silky mane.

Now that he was back on board, Altivo put the idea of having fun out of his mind. After all, he was about to journey to the New World. He had to be ready to serve his master.

But Altivo did wish that Cortes would give him a *little* more to eat. Lately his master had been feeding the poor horse less than usual so he would be in top shape.

"Hey, Altivo!" cried a sailor as he passed with a basket of bright red apples.

Mmmm. Altivo loved apples. He stretched his neck out as far as he could and tried to grab one with his teeth. The horse was hungry. If he could just nab one apple . . .

But the sailor pulled the basket away. "Not for you. You're on half rations!" he called out.

Plunk! One of the apples fell out of the basket. Thrilled, Altivo moved toward it. But before he could get it, it rolled away and disappeared through a wooden grate in the floor.

Altivo snorted in disappointment and tried not to think about his growling stomach and that beautiful, tasty apple.

He peered through the grate, but all he could see was darkness. But he did *hear* something—two men's voices and a banging sound.

"So, um . . . how's the escape plan coming, Tulio? We've got to get out of here," said one of the men.

Bang! Bang Bang! "All right, all right. Wait! I'm getting something," said Tulio, who was banging his head against the wall, hoping it would help him think better.

Altivo thought the voices sounded familiar. Where had he heard them before? Then he remembered. They were the voices of the two men he had seen playing dice in town. They must have been

captured by Cortes's men.

"Okay, here is the plan, Miguel," said Tulio. "In the dead of night you and I grab some supplies, hijack one of those longboats, and row back to Spain."

"Back to Spain?" asked Miguel.

"Yeah," said Tulio.

"In a rowboat?"

"You got it!"

"So that's your plan?" said Miguel.

"That's pretty much it," said Tulio.

"So how do we get on deck?"

The men paused and thought about this problem. As they thought, the only sounds on the quiet ship were Altivo's hoof beats as he walked across the deck.

"Wait! I have an idea!" Miguel cried. "Give me a boost!"

CHAPTER FOUR

A SMART HORSE

"H ey, Altivo . . . here, Altivo!" Miguel whispered. Altivo saw two hands rise up through the grate. They were tossing something around, back and forth, back and forth. It was the apple that had rolled away!

"You want a nice apple? Come and get it!" Miguel continued.

Altivo was delighted, for that apple looked good! He trotted over to the grate and leaned down to get it. But the hand that was holding it quickly drew away.

Altivo whinnied angrily. How dare anyone try to fool him, the great warhorse!

"You have to do a trick for me first," said Miguel.

Altivo peered through the grate again.

"All you have to do is find a pry bar!" Miguel told

him. "You know, a long piece of iron with a hooky thing at the end, yeah?"

"Miguel, you're talking to a horse!" Tulio whispered.

"Shush!" said Miguel, who seemed sure of what he was doing. "That's it, Altivo! Find the pry bar!"

"Yes, find the pry bar," said Tulio with a snicker. "He can't understand *pry bar*. He's a dumb horse. There's no way . . ."

Altivo snorted. Didn't they know who he was? Didn't they know they were talking to one of the smartest horses around? They wanted a pry bar?

He'd give them something even better!

Altivo knew just what to do. He lifted a ring of keys off a hook with his teeth and dropped it through the grate.

Clank! The keys landed neatly on the ground. Miguel and Tulio were silent for a moment.

"Well, it's not a pry bar," said Tulio as he shook his head and picked up the keys.

CHAPTER FIVE

OVERBOARD!

That evening, Altivo watched as first Miguel, then Tulio, appeared on deck. It was time for their escape!

Tulio glanced around quickly for some food to take with them. All he could spot was a sack of apples, which was better than nothing. So he grabbed it and headed on tiptoe for a lifeboat.

Meanwhile, Altivo nuzzled Miguel's pocket, still trying to get that juicy apple.

"Oh, Altivo. Oh, thank you. Listen, if we can ever return the favor . . ." said Miguel as he patted Altivo on the nose.

Altivo looked down at him wide-eyed. He had never been spoken to with such kindness before. But Miguel seemed to have forgotten about the apple. And Altivo still *really* wanted it.

"Oh, for Pete's sake, Miguel," Tulio said with a moan. "He's a ruthless warhorse, not a poodle! Come on, before he licks you to death!"

With that, both men settled themselves in the boat and began to lower it. Down, down, down it went, over the side of the ship.

Altivo watched the boat as it slipped farther and farther away. All hope of getting that apple seemed to be slipping away right with it. And so did all hope of getting to know these two fellows, who seemed much nicer than Cortes.

Altivo rushed over to the rail. "*Neigh!*" he cried. It was as if he were calling out "No!"

"*Shhh!*" called Miguel.

"*Neigh!*" whined Altivo again, a little more loudly this time.

"What's the matter with him?" cried Tulio.

"He wants his apple," said Miguel.

"Well, give it to him before he wakes up the whole ship!" whispered Tulio angrily. He grabbed the apple from Miguel and threw it to the horse. "Fetch!"

But Tulio never did have very good aim. Altivo watched helplessly as the apple arched right over his head and bounced off a sail. Then it hit a mast and knocked into a telescope. Finally, it bounced high into the air and flew overboard, straight down into the ocean.

Altivo stared as the juicy treat he'd been craving hit the water. Without stopping to think, he leapt over the side rail and plunged into the ocean after the apple.

There was only one problem. He didn't know how to swim!

CHAPTER SIX

A LOSING BATTLE

Altivo hit the water with a great splash. It drenched Tulio and Miguel, who were still suspended halfway down the side of the ship in their swinging lifeboat.

"Altivo!" Miguel yelled. He leaped up and dove into the water from the hanging boat. He had seen at once that the poor horse could not swim.

"Miguel! *Miguel!*" yelled Tulio. He lost hold of the rope that was suspending the boat in the air. "AHHHHH!" he yelled as the boat flew down the side of the ship and hit the water.

Tulio began rowing madly over to his friend.

"Altivo! I'm coming!" screamed Miguel.

But Altivo didn't even hear his words. He was too busy fighting the massive ocean and gasping for air.

"Miguel!" yelled Tulio.

"Hang on! I'm right here, old boy!" Miguel shouted to the horse.

"Have you lost your mind?" screamed Tulio to Miguel.

Altivo desperately tried to hold his breath each time he plunged underwater. But even so he felt he was swallowing gallons of seawater. Every time he came up he spat out as much as he could.

The frantic horse felt as if he were in battle once again. But this was far worse than any battle he had ever fought with Cortes. And worst of all, he felt he was losing—for the first time in his life.

"Help is coming," cried Miguel.

Altivo spat out another mouthful of water and

gasped before he sank once more beneath the surface. But this time he heard Miguel's words. He was trying to save his life! With new strength, Altivo heaved himself above the surface of the water. He gasped for yet another breath of air.

But just then a large shadow fell over the struggling group. An enormous ship was headed right for them—the next in line of Cortes's fleet. It passed safely by, but within seconds a gigantic wave from the wake of the ship hit Altivo. It knocked the lifeboat over, and sent all three adventurers—and most of the apples—plunging deep into the sea.

CHAPTER SEVEN

RESCUED!

Altivo popped his head up out of the water and gasped for air. He sensed something over his head and realized that it was their boat, upside down now. He was trapped under it!

"Loop the rope under the horse!" Tulio cried out.

Altivo saw Miguel swimming under him and wondered what he was doing. Miguel quickly looped a rope around the horse's body. He and Tulio climbed up on top of the upside-down boat and tied the rope to it.

Altivo became frightened as the rope tightened around him, and he began thrashing wildly in the water.

"On the count of three, pull back on the rope!" Tulio shouted.

"What?"

At that moment, Tulio spotted another ship looming over them.

"Three! Pull!" he shouted.

The ship created a giant wave, which helped turn the little boat right-side up again—and sent Miguel and Tulio plunging back into the water.

Meanwhile Altivo felt a huge force heaving him *out* of the water. The next thing he knew he was in the boat, staring at the silent night sky—and his hooves were sticking straight up into the air!

I'm alive! he thought. Quickly, he turned himself over, making sure not to tip the boat. As he did this, a bright red apple rolled across the wooden floor—and then another, and another. He saw a couple more wedged under a seat. Delighted, Altivo began munching on apple after apple.

Suddenly the horse stopped eating. Where were Miguel and Tulio? Altivo's heart beat fast for a moment. But soon he saw them swimming toward the boat, and his fears disappeared.

Altivo was thrilled to have Miguel and Tulio safely in the boat with him. Suddenly he realized these were his friends—not his masters, but his friends. After all, they had just saved his life!

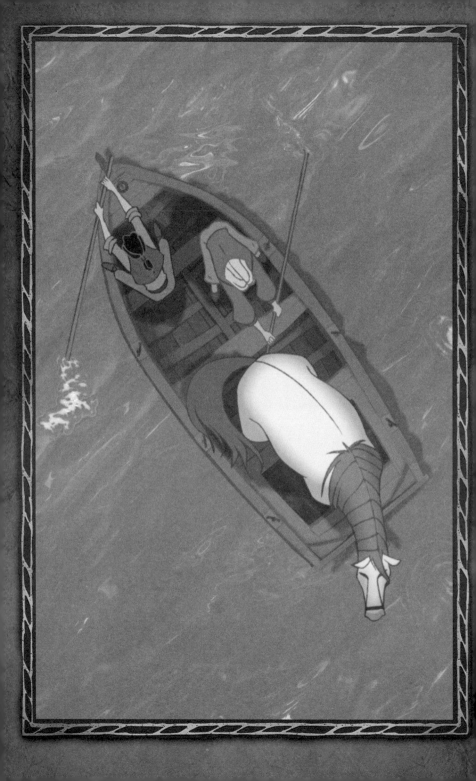

Chapter Eight

Lost at Sea

"Here we are—hey, it worked!" cried Miguel. The two men climbed into the boat and flopped down to catch their breath.

"Did any of the supplies make it?" asked Tulio, looking around.

"Well, um, yes and no," said Miguel as he looked closely at Altivo.

The horse's cheeks were bulging with the apples, and he gave the two men a guilty look.

"Ooooooh . . . great!" Tulio sighed.

"Tulio, look on the positive side," said Miguel. "At least things can't get any—"

Suddenly the sky seemed to crack wide open and heavy rain came pouring down.

"Were you going to say *worse*?" asked Tulio.

Water was everywhere—not only in the ocean

now, but in the boat and all over the three travelers
as well.

CRASH! Thunder echoed over the waves.
Lightning filled the sky. Miguel, Tulio, and Altivo
huddled together, partly for warmth, but mainly for
comfort.

Yes, things *were* getting worse. Altivo shivered.
His beautiful coat was soaking wet. His mane hung
on his neck like a wet rag. He moved even closer to
his new friends. True, he was wet. He was cold. Yet
somehow, he felt he would be okay. And he felt
that Miguel and Tulio really needed him. These two
bumbling guys needed *someone* with some sense on

board! Yes, they would all be okay. After all, they were a team now.

Day after day passed with no land in sight. Day after day, all Altivo saw for miles around was blue water and a bluer sky. The sun beat down on them mercilessly. Their stomachs growled with hunger, and their water supply was running dangerously low.

One day, an exhausted seagull landed on the boat. Tulio and Miguel's eyes lit up with hope and relief. *Food!* Quickly, Tulio reached out to capture the bird. But before he could get near, a shark leaped out of the water and slammed its jaws around the poor creature.

Tulio let out an anguished sob.

Altivo wondered what else could possibly go wrong. Just what had he gotten himself into?

CHAPTER NINE

"IT'S LAAAAAND!"

One week passed and then two. Still the two men and the horse floated on the ocean in their little boat, with no land in sight. They slumped wearily against one another, having nearly lost hope.

"Tulio, did you ever imagine it would end like this?" asked Miguel.

"The horse is a surprise," answered Tulio.

Altivo's ears perked up.

"Any regrets?" asked Miguel.

"Besides dying, yeah," said his buddy. "I never had enough gold."

Altivo couldn't believe they were thinking of gold again. How could they have gold on their minds when they were close to starvation?

"My regret—besides dying," said Miguel, "is that our greatest adventure is over before it began. And no one will even remember us. Where's the glory in that?"

"Well, if it makes you feel any better, Miguel, you made my life an adventure," said Tulio.

"And if it makes *you* feel any better, Tulio, you made my life rich," added Miguel.

Altivo rolled his eyes. Sometimes humans could be so silly.

Soon the three travelers could not keep their eyes open. The ocean water lapped up gently against Miguel and Tulio's hands, which hung over the side of the boat. Slowly, everyone fell asleep. Tulio and Miguel dreamed of mountains of gold, while Altivo dreamed of apples, sugar cubes, and fresh hay.

While they slept, the boat drifted with the waves, making its way to wherever the tide would take it.

Everyone awoke at once, for the boat no longer seemed to be rocking like a cradle. Miguel and Tulio lifted their hands. They were filled with sand!

"Is it . . . ?" cried Miguel.

"It is!" answered Tulio.

Altivo looked around, blinked, and then looked again.

"It's . . . it's . . . it's laaaaand!" Miguel and Tulio cried out together.

The three adventurers tumbled out of the boat and began kissing the sand.

But suddenly Altivo saw something that made his mane stand up straight on his neck. Lying in the sand was a skeleton, with a war club still in its skull and a sword through its rib cage!

"Ahhhhhh!" screamed Tulio and Miguel, for they had seen it too.

"All in favor of getting back in the boat, say aye!" Tulio cried.

"Aye!" Miguel and Tulio called out together.

Altivo whinnied in agreement.

"Let's go," ordered Tulio, and he turned and headed back to the boat.

But all at once Miguel stopped short. He noticed something in the near distance. It looked familiar. He squinted and thought. Then he smiled.

CHAPTER TEN

THE MAP

"Miguel!" cried Tulio, back at the boat. "I could use a little help.... Miguel? Hello?"

Tulio and Altivo turned and spotted Miguel still standing on the beach. His gaze moved back and forth between a large rock and a piece of paper in his hand. And he had a huge grin on his face.

"Tulio!" he called out. "We've done it!"

"What's that?" said Tulio. "The map?"

"It's all right here!" yelled Miguel. He held up the map and waved it in the air.

"You still have the *map*?" Tulio cried in amazement.

"The whistling rock ... the stream ..." said Miguel. He could barely get his breath.

"You kept the map, but you couldn't grab a little more food?" shouted Tulio.

Hmmmm. Altivo thought he had a point.

"Even those mountains! You said so yourself. It *could* be possible—and it *is*! It really is the map to El Dorado!" cried Miguel.

"You drank seawater, didn't you?" muttered Tulio as he shook his head.

"Come on!" cried Miguel, his eyes opening as wide as the stretch of sand around them.

"I'm not coming on!" yelled Tulio. "I wouldn't set foot in that jungle for a million pesetas."

"How about a hundred million?" asked Miguel. He lifted his eyebrows, tipped his head, and smiled.

"What?" said Tulio.

Miguel began to roll up the map.

"I just thought that, after all, since El Dorado is the city of gold . . ." he said.

"What's your point?" asked Tulio.

"You know," said Miguel with a shrug. "Dust, nuggets, bricks. A temple of gold where you can pluck gold from the very walls. But you don't want to go. So let's get back in the boat and row back to Spain. After all, it worked so well last time. . . ."

"Wait. . . . Wait a minute," said Tulio. "New plan. We find the city of gold . . ."

Oh, no! Altivo snorted.

"...we take the gold...*then* we go back to
Spain..."

"And buy Spain!" shouted Miguel.

"Yeah!" said Tulio.

Altivo didn't think he liked this plan at all.
Floating around in the ocean wasn't great. But it
had to be better than ending up as a skeleton on a
beach with a war club in your head, didn't it?

"Come on, Tulio. We'll follow that trail!" cried
Miguel.

"What trail?" asked Tulio.

"The trail that we blaze!" cried Miguel. He
grabbed the sword from the skeleton and began

hacking away at the dense branches. Then he
motioned for his friends to follow.

Altivo smelled danger. He'd been in enough bat-
tles to know that smell and to know it well. But his
friends seemed so excited. How could he leave
them on their own now? They would be lost without him—even with that map. And the truth was . . .
he'd be lost without them. After all, they were the
first real friends he had ever had.

And so the three adventurers headed into the
jungle.

CHAPTER ELEVEN

THROUGH THE JUNGLE

Altivo trotted along proudly with Miguel and Tulio on his back. The jungle air felt cool. For the first time in nearly two weeks the sun did not beat down on the travelers' weary bodies. Shafts of sunlight made their way through, but only where the leaves were less dense.

And everything in the jungle was so big! Altivo had never seen such tall trees. Nor had he seen such wide trunks. The bases spread out like the fingers of a mammoth hand, with cozy nesting places in between. Suddenly the big, strong warhorse felt very small.

Birds sang softly in the trees. The only other sound was the clip-clop of Altivo's hooves making their way gently over the soft earth.

But suddenly the branches in front of the horse

rustled. Something was moving quickly through the leaves. Altivo stopped short. A snake! It was chasing a small animal—an armadillo. Miguel leaped off the horse and stabbed the snake with his sword. The armadillo was saved!

Grateful to Miguel for saving his life, the little creature just couldn't say good-bye. So he tagged along behind them.

Altivo looked around as he walked and gave a small neigh. He had dreamed of a life of freedom and adventure. And here it was! The skeleton on the beach seemed very far away now. How could anything bad happen in such a beautiful place?

Tulio and Miguel seemed to be feeling the same way. "Charge!" yelled Miguel, flying along on

Altivo's back and feeling the sheer joy of their adventure.

As they continued along their way, Tulio and Miguel began to sing. How much nicer it was listening to songs than to rude commands from Cortes! Now, *this* was the life!

One by one, the team began discovering the landmarks that were on the map. They spotted a large group of rocks with light streaming through.

The light cast a shadow in the eerie shape of a flying skull. Sure enough, there was a picture of a skull right on the map! They must be going the right way!

On they walked, looking for clues and blazing their trail. After some time they came to a rushing stream. Jutting out of the water was a rock with a picture carved into the side of it. Tulio looked closer—it was a picture of a fish, just like the one on the map! That meant they were still going the right way.

But they had to get across the stream. Carefully,

Miguel, Altivo, and Tulio stepped from stone to stone, making their way to the other side. But just as they were about to step back on land, a fish leaped out of the water—and nipped poor Tulio on his behind! He nearly fell into the water.

Everyone was happy to finally get back on dry land. They traveled on, pushing through the lush vegetation. Butterflies of every color flitted around their heads. Ferns grew so tall that they tickled Altivo's nose as he trotted along. A busy little colony of leaf-cutter ants marched in a straight line across his path. Altivo carefully stepped around so as not to disturb them as they carried their heavy loads of bits of leaves.

The next moment Altivo whinnied, for he had found a treat for them all—a bubbling hot spring! He jumped in with a great splash and whinnied for his friends to follow. Tulio and Miguel threw off their clothes and leaped into the refreshing pool. All their cares and worries seemed to slip away and dissolve within seconds. A bath had never felt so good!

But suddenly little chattering sounds caught their attention. Altivo turned to see two little monkeys running rapidly through the dense growth. They darted up a tree and down again and swung happily on the branches. But what was that one of them was wearing?

"Hey, my pants!" cried Tulio as the monkey slipped away. Poor Tulio leaped out of the water and chased after the pesky little fellow. Miguel burst into laughter, for Tulio was quite a sight as he ran through the trees.

But the joke was on Miguel! No sooner did he start laughing than another monkey grabbed *his* clothes! Altivo gave a giant snort.

The two men finally got their clothes back, and the frisky monkeys disappeared into the underbrush.

Altivo had never had such fun in his life. He even enjoyed finding shelter under a tropical leaf when an afternoon storm broke out. The leaf was large enough to protect all three hikers at once!

After the storm, the wet leaves and flowers sparkled in the sunlight as it shone through spaces in the thick canopy. Bright orchids gave off an aroma that made Altivo think of the best sugar cubes.

The trail began to slope steeply upward, and Miguel and Tulio grew weary. They walked behind Altivo, holding on to his tail for support.

Altivo was tired as well, but he trotted along quite merrily. Moving to a steady rhythm, he put one hoof in front of the other. Left, right, left—

"Whoa!" Tulio shrieked. But it was too late.

Altivo's foot kept going straight down, through the air. He and his friends tumbled down a steep ravine and landed with a loud *thump!*

CHAPTER TWELVE

A GREAT BIG ROCK

Altivo opened his eyes. *Oooh*, he ached. Next to him, Tulio was shaking Miguel furiously and holding up the map.

"Miguel, Miguel . . . wake up! We're there!"

"We've found it?" asked Miguel in a sleepy voice.

Altivo snorted and looked around. Right in front of him was a great big rock—a large monolith. It looked just like the picture on the map. But there was no city of gold. There was just a rushing waterfall and more jungle.

"Oh, yeah," said Tulio. "We've found it."

"Fantastic! Where is it?" asked Miguel. "Behind the rock?"

"No, no," said Tulio. "This is it. The rock." With a grand gesture, he pointed at the monolith. "Welcome to El Dorado!" he said mockingly.

Altivo and Miguel stared at the giant black monolith. This was El Dorado? It couldn't be. Where was the gold? Where were the riches?

Miguel's face fell in disbelief.

Altivo snorted loudly. He didn't care about the gold. But he did care about Miguel and Tulio. And if they wanted gold, he wanted it for them.

"Give me that!" cried Miguel, grabbing the map from Tulio.

"I guess El Dorado is native for GREAT BIG ROOOCK!" Tulio yelled. And he climbed onto Altivo's back.

"You don't think Cortes could have gotten here before us and . . . ?" said Miguel.

"And what?" cried Tulio. "Taken all the really *big* rocks?"

Altivo jerked the reins when he heard Cortes's

name. He was furious at the thought that Cortes could have gotten to El Dorado before his friends. Now he knew, without a doubt, that he would never return to his old master. Not now. Not if he could help it. All his old feelings of duty were gone. In their place were much stronger feelings of loyalty to the first real friends he had ever had.

Tulio pulled the reins to turn Altivo away from the monolith. He was giving up! Altivo couldn't believe it.

"Tulio, we have to think about this," said Miguel. "I mean, we've come all this way and we should really . . ."

"Get on the horse! We're leaving!" cried Tulio.

Miguel sighed. He climbed up and joined Tulio on Altivo's back.

Chapter Thirteen

El Dorado!

Altivo waited patiently as Miguel and Tulio stared down at the map. They were trying to figure out how to get back to the shore.

"It looks like there's a pass right over there . . ." said Tulio.

But he never finished his sentence, for just at that moment a figure burst through the waterfall behind them. A beautiful young woman with long streaming black hair ran straight into Altivo. She was being chased by a troop of soldiers carrying long spears. Startled, Altivo whinnied and reared up.

"Hello," said Tulio nervously. "Is this your rock? Sorry. We were just looking. We're tourists . . . tour-ists. We . . . we lost our tour group. May we go now?"

The soldiers didn't answer. They captured the young woman and motioned for Tulio, Miguel, and Altivo to come with them as well. The little armadillo followed close behind.

Altivo wondered where the soldiers could be taking them.

The soldiers led them behind the waterfall and into a dark tunnel through which a roaring river ran. Ice-cold water sprayed against their faces, and the sound of the waterfall was nearly deafening.

The soldiers herded them into a boat and steered it through an ancient stone gateway. It was so dark that Altivo could barely see. But as the boat turned a corner, sunlight came streaming in. Altivo blinked and looked down, for the brightness burned his eyes.

When he looked up he beheld a most amazing

sight—a city of gold. *The* city of gold. It was more than he could have ever imagined. Bright sunlight bounced off the buildings, creating a gleaming, sparkling spectacle.

Altivo had never seen such a sight in his life—or so much gold. He was truly dazzled. The sidewalks were gold. The people hurrying through the streets wore gold—gold bracelets, gold earrings, gold rings on every finger.

Tulio and Miguel sat and stared in wonder. Even the buildings were golden. Most amazing of all was a majestic gold temple, shaped like a pyramid. It seemed to cast a golden glow over everything in sight.

Altivo neighed in delight.

"It's . . . it's . . . it's El Dorado!" cried Miguel, Tulio, and Altivo.

Indeed it was. They had found the lost city of El Dorado.

And they had done it all together. As a team. Who knew what adventure awaited them next?

Altivo raised his head high. His friends had found their gold. And he had helped them do it. As for him—he had found something as good as gold. *Or better!* he thought, as he looked at his friends and whinnied.